KIRSTEN
SNOWBOUND!

BY JANET SHAW

ILLUSTRATIONS RENÉE GRAEF

VIGNETTES SUSAN MCALILEY

THE AMERICAN GIRLS COLLECTION®

Published by Pleasant Company Publications
Previously published in *American Girl*® magazine
© Copyright 2001 by Pleasant Company
For information, address: Book Editor, Pleasant Company Publications,
8400 Fairway Place, P.O. Box 620998, Middleton, WI 53562.

Printed in Singapore.
01 02 03 04 05 06 07 08 TWP 10 9 8 7 6 5 4 3 2 1

Edited by Nancy Holyoke, Michelle Jones, and Michelle N. Watkins
Designed by Joshua Mjaanes and Laura Moberly
Art Directed by Kym Abrams and Joshua Mjaanes

Library of Congress Cataloging-in-Publication Data

Shaw, Janet Beeler, 1937-
Kirsten snowbound! / by Janet Shaw ;
illustrations, Renée Graef ; vignettes, Susan McAliley.
p. cm. — (The American girls collection)
Summary: In 1856, Kirsten and her cousins look after the farm
while the adults go to town for supplies and everything is fine—
until a blizzard surprises them.

ISBN 1-58485-273-9
[1. Blizzards—Fiction. 2. Swedish Americans—Fiction.
3. Cousins—Fiction. 4. Frontier and pioneer life—Minnesota—Fiction.
5. Minnesota—Fiction.]
I. Graef, Renée, ill. II. McAliley, Susan, ill. III. Title. IV. Series
PZ7.S53423 Kis 2001   [Fic]—dc21   00-032653

The
AMERICAN GIRLS
COLLECTION
®

OTHER AMERICAN GIRLS
SHORT STORIES:

FELICITY TAKES A DARE

JOSEFINA'S SONG

ADDY'S WEDDING QUILT

SAMANTHA AND THE
MISSING PEARLS

MOLLY MARCHES ON

PICTURE CREDITS

The following individuals and organizations have generously given
permission to reprint illustrations contained in "Looking Back":
p. 33—Courtesy Lyon & Healy; p. 34—Courtesy of Bloomingdale's Department
Stores, *Bloomingdale's Illustrated 1886 Catalog*, Dover Publications, Inc.; p. 39—Hires
root beer is a registered trademark of Dr Pepper/Seven Up, Inc. © 2000; p. 40—
Photography by Jamie Young and prop styling by Jean doPico; p. 43—From *Michael
Hague's Favorite Hans Christian Andersen Family Tales*, illustrated by Michael
Hague, illustrations © 1981 by Michael Hague, reprinted by permission of
Henry Holt & Company, LLC; p. 45—Illustrations by Geri Bourget;
pp. 46–48—Illustrations by D. J. Simison.

TABLE OF CONTENTS

PAPA
*Kirsten's father, who
is sometimes gruff
but always loving.*

MAMA
*Kirsten's mother, who
never loses heart.*

KIRSTEN
*A ten-year-old
who moves with her
family to a new
home on America's
frontier in 1854.*

LARS
*Kirsten's sixteen-year-old
brother, who is
almost a man.*

PETER
*Kirsten's mischievous
brother, who is
seven years old.*

BRITTA
*Kirsten's baby sister,
who is eleven months old.*

LISBETH
*Kirsten's thirteen-year-old
cousin.*

ANNA
*Kirsten's nine-year-old
cousin.*

KIRSTEN
SNOWBOUND!

"Tonight we'll have fresh bread again!" Kirsten said. "I've almost forgotten how good it tastes." She held baby Britta on her hip as she watched Mama, Aunt Inger, and her big brother, Lars, drive away in the wagon.

"And rice porridge, too!" said Kirsten's cousin Anna. "I'm so tired of eating wrinkly potatoes!"

"But we should be thankful to have them," cousin Lisbeth added. That's

1

what Aunt Inger always said when she put the potatoes into the pot to boil.

It was April, and old potatoes were about all the Larsons had to eat. They'd used up most of the supplies they'd bought last fall. They hadn't been able to buy more because all winter long the road to town had been too muddy for the wagon to travel on. But now at last the road was dry. Lars was driving Mama and Aunt Inger to the store, where they would buy flour, sugar, salt, coffee, rice, and many other things. Kirsten, her cousins, and her little brother, Peter, would look after the farm until the others came home that night.

With the adults gone, there was lots

of work to do! Peter fed the chickens and cleaned the barn. Anna swept out the cabin that the two families shared. Lisbeth fed Britta, changed her, and washed her diapers. Kirsten drove the cows in from the field and milked them.

As Kirsten worked, she rested her head against the cow's warm side and imagined the delicious scent of ginger and the other spices Mama would buy. And maybe she'd bring a letter from Papa telling when he'd be home from the logging camp. Kirsten couldn't wait to see the wagon coming back down the road that evening.

3

Big flakes of snow spattered Kirsten's face when she stepped outside the barn. While she'd been inside milking the cows, dark clouds had covered the sky and a strong wind had come up. *But this is spring snow,* she thought. *Surely it will melt as quickly as it falls.*

By midday the wind had become a powerful gale and snow fell hard and fast. Kirsten and the others bundled into thick sweaters and gathered by the fireplace to keep warm while they ate the potato soup Aunt Inger had left for them.

"The old woman in the sky is picking feathers from her goose!" Anna said about the snow, and Peter laughed.

But Kirsten remembered being lost

in the snowstorm with Papa. If Mama
and the others were out in the storm,
they were in danger.

"I wish the wagon were coming
down our road right now," Kirsten said.

Peter went to the window. He had to
stand on tiptoe to peek over the snow
piled on the sill. "I can't see the road any-
more," he said. "I can barely see the barn."

Lisbeth frowned. "They would
never try to drive home if they couldn't
see the road. Maybe they'll stay with
friends in town tonight."

"I wouldn't like it if Mama didn't
come home tonight," Peter said. "We'd
be alone."

"But we're not alone! There are five

of us, counting Britta," Anna said. "I
think it would be an adventure!"

"I just hope the snow stops soon,"
Kirsten said. She went to the window with
Peter. As she looked out, the barn vanished
behind a whirling curtain of snow.

Snow fell more and more thickly.
Trees bent in the wind, and snow-covered

branches broke and crashed to the ground. The cabin trembled and shook. Snow hissed in through the chinks between the logs of the cabin walls. It blew in through the cracks around the door and the windows, and collected in drifts on the wooden floor. Kirsten and Lisbeth took turns sweeping it up.

"I've never seen such a big blizzard!" Lisbeth said.

Peter sat hugging his knees by the fire, his eyes wide. "What's a blizzard?"

"A fierce storm like this one," Anna said. She bared her teeth and made a scary face to tease him. "An enormous snowstorm that won't stop!"

"Don't say that!" Peter looked as though he might cry.

Kirsten tugged his ear. "Peter, don't be frightened," she said. "We're safe here in the cabin, and the others are safe in town."

But are the others safe? Kirsten wondered as the wind wailed more loudly. *In a blizzard like this one, can anyone be safe, even in a cabin?*

It was late afternoon when Kirsten heard something scratch roughly at the door.

"What could be there?" Peter asked. "A wolf?"

"Maybe someone's lost in the storm

and saw our light," Anna said.

The thing scratched harder. And barked!

"It's Caro!" Kirsten cried. "He's cold and wants in." She ran to let the dog inside.

Kirsten tugged the door open. The fierce wind tore it from her grip and slammed it against the wall. Caro ran inside as a cloud of snow rushed into the cabin through the open doorway.

"The blizzard's coming inside!" Peter cried.

"Shut the door!" Lisbeth shouted over the roar of the wind. As she pulled at the door, the wind broke the wooden hinge at the top. Anna rushed to help her

"The blizzard's coming inside!" Peter cried.

sister hold the door steady so the bottom hinge wouldn't break, too.

Baby Britta began to cry in the icy wind. Kirsten moved to pick her up, but Anna cried, "Kirsten, help us first! There's so much snow on the floor that we can't push the door shut!"

Kirsten grabbed the broom, but the wind snatched it from her and knocked it across the floor. Then she bent and swept at the deepening drift with her skirt. Snow was thick in her eyelashes and hair.

Peter snatched up the empty soup pot. He scooped up some snow, but when he threw it outside, the wind blew it back into his face.

"If we can't get the snow out, we'll

have to shovel it farther inside!" Kirsten cried. She ran for the shovel by the fireplace. At the door again, she turned her back to the wind and dug into the snow, throwing it away from the path of the door. "Help me, Peter!" she called. He crouched and scooped aside the snow with the pot until they could see the floor.

Then Kirsten, Peter, Lisbeth, and Anna all got behind the door and pushed. At last, in spite of the wind, they forced the door shut. Kirsten's hand shook as she latched it.

"This door won't stay shut with a broken hinge," Lisbeth said. "Can we nail it shut?"

Britta was crying so hard she had

hiccups, but Kirsten couldn't stop to comfort her. She ran to get the hammer and nails. Then she pounded nails in around the edge of the door until it was braced firmly in place.

By the time Kirsten finished, they were all trembling with cold. She grabbed up Britta from her cradle and carried her near the fire. "Hush now, hush-a-baby," she murmured.

Kirsten's teeth chattered as she hugged the baby to her shoulder. The others looked at her silently. "It was a mistake to open the door," she said slowly. "But I had to let Caro in. He would have frozen to death outside."

13

"We'd all be frozen if we hadn't got the door shut," Lisbeth said. She brushed snow off her clothes, then used the broom to sweep snow off Peter and Anna. "We have to be very careful so we don't make any more mistakes."

Peter hugged his elbows. "Kirsten, what would Mama do if she were here now?"

Kirsten stroked Britta's cold cheek. "If Mama were here, she'd tell us to help each other so we'd be safe," she said. Her voice was soft. "She'd tell us to think things through."

"You're right, Kirsten. We have to have a plan," Lisbeth said gently. She held her hands close to the fire to warm

14

them. "To begin with, we need to keep a fire going during the night."

Kirsten nodded. "And we'll stay much warmer if we get into bed now."

"We'll sleep wearing all our flannel petticoats and our sweaters and shawls and even our mittens," Anna said, smiling.

"We'll snuggle Britta in with us," Kirsten added. "And we'll push the bed near the fireplace for extra warmth. Let's do that first."

Quickly they pushed the bed in front of the fireplace and piled all the blankets on it. Peter and Anna crawled in. Kirsten tugged Britta's cap on, tucked her in, and lay down beside her. Lisbeth put more wood on the fire and got in on the other side of the bed. They pulled the thick cotton sheet over their heads to keep off the snow blowing in through the cracks.

"Don't let Britta crawl out from under the blankets," Kirsten said.

"And don't roll on top of her," Lisbeth added.

"I can't roll at all!" Anna said. "I can't even wiggle my toes. We're like bear cubs crowded into a little den. Isn't this exciting!"

But Kirsten wasn't excited. She was scared! *What if the wind topples the cabin over?* she thought. *What if the wind blows the roof off? What if a tree falls on the cabin*

*and crushes it? What if Mama and the others
are lost in this terrible blizzard and never
come home at all?*

Kirsten was dreaming someone was
pricking her fingers with needles. She
woke and clenched her hand. As she slept,
her arm had slipped out from under the
blankets. Now her hand lay in snow that
had blown onto the bedcovers. Snow
stung her fingers, but her body was numb
with cold. She pulled the icy sheet from
her face and sat up.

The lamp had gone out, but a faint
light came through the snow-covered
windows. The fire had burned down to

gray coals, and the cabin was bitter cold. Peter and Anna were sleeping. Lisbeth was sleeping, too. Kirsten could see clouds of breath at their lips. Was Britta warm enough?

Kirsten reached for the baby. But Britta wasn't there! Kirsten scrambled out of bed and began to search. *Had Britta crawled down under the heavy covers? Had she smothered with not enough air to breathe?* Kirsten felt all over the bed, but she couldn't find Britta anywhere. Her heart sped with fear.

"Lisbeth!" Kirsten hissed. "Wake up! Britta's gone!"

Right away Lisbeth jumped out of bed. "She can crawl, but she can't have gone far!" Lisbeth said.

"But if she's not under the blankets, she could be frozen!" Kirsten said.

Now Anna and Peter were awake, too. They looked under the pillow, as if Britta might be hidden there. "Here's one of her mittens!" Anna said.

Kirsten peered under a blanket rumpled at the foot of the bed. No Britta. Then Kirsten went down on her knees to look under the bed. Another blanket had fallen there and lay in a heap. Caro slept on the crumpled blanket. And there, sleeping half-hidden by the curve of his body, was the baby!

Kirsten touched Britta's cheek. It was warm from Caro's thick fur. "She's here!

She's all right!"

Lisbeth went down on her knees, too. She reached for Britta. "Even her hands are warm!"

"It's a good thing I let Caro in!" Kirsten said. She gathered Britta into her arms and kissed her soft cheek. "You're a lucky baby, Britta. Our dog saved your life."

Caro wagged his tail, as though he knew he'd done something good. Lisbeth patted the bed. "Jump up here, Caro. Keep everyone warm while we build a good fire."

Kirsten went to the shed off the kitchen to get more wood for the fire, but there were only three pieces and some hay left in the wood box.

Her heart sank. "We don't have enough wood to build a good fire, Lisbeth," she said. "There's more wood outside, but we'll never find it under the snow."

Lisbeth was pulling on her boots. "If we don't panic, we'll think of something," she said.

21

"Yes, if we think things through we'll be all right," Kirsten said softly. As she looked around the cabin, she got an idea. "I know! We can burn the stools and the bench. That dry wood will make a hot fire."

"Mama won't like it if we burn her bench," Anna said.

"Anna, we have to keep warm to stay alive," Kirsten said.

"And Papa can make another bench," Peter added. "He can make lots of benches."

Kirsten took some hay and twisted it into thin strands. She lay the strands on the gray coals and blew on them gently. Soon small flames caught in the hay. When the hay was burning,

Kirsten put the last three pieces of wood on it. Lisbeth knocked the legs off the smallest stool with the hammer. She put them on the fire, too. The dry wood quickly caught and blazed up.

"It works!" Peter said. "We can burn the trundle bed, if we have to. We can burn our skis and even the table."

"I'm a little warmer already," Anna said. "Is there anything to eat?"

Kirsten looked into the water bucket. The water was solid ice. She set the bucket by the fire to melt it. The milk was frozen, too. "We can melt the milk for Britta," Kirsten said. "And we can melt ice so we'll have water to drink. But there's nothing to eat, Anna."

"Aren't there some more wrinkly potatoes?" Anna asked. "I really don't mind wrinkly potatoes."

"We've eaten the last of the potatoes," Lisbeth said. She was poking around in the cupboard, lifting the lids off boxes and jars. "But here's a handful of dried beans! When the water melts, we can boil them."

"Beans," Anna said sadly. "Well, I really don't mind beans."

Kirsten used a wooden spoon to scrape the thick ice from the windowpane. When she got a space cleared, she peered out. The snow had stopped falling, and the wind wasn't blowing. Rays of sun shone

24

across the frozen white fields. But she could hardly recognize the farm! Snow had drifted up to the roof of the barn. Huge branches lay on the snow around the cabin. The fences were buried in drifts, and ice covered the road. Although on this side of the cabin the snow was only as high as the window, they were snowbound.

Lisbeth joined Kirsten at the window and peeked through the hole. "Do you think we can shovel our way to the barn?" she asked.

"We'll have to try," Kirsten said. "The animals need to be looked after, and it might be a long time before the others come home." She put her lips next to

Lisbeth's ear. "They *will* come home, won't they?" she whispered.

Lisbeth clasped Kirsten's hand in hers. "Our plan is to dig a path to the barn. Let's not think about anything else."

They pried the nails out of the door with the hammer and wedge. When Kirsten pulled the door open, she saw snow piled as high as her chest. She shoveled away enough so she and Lisbeth could wade outside and shut the door.

Kirsten and Lisbeth took turns digging with the shovel and the soup pot. The snow was heavy and hard to lift. After what seemed like ages, Kirsten looked back at the house to see how far they'd come. It was only a little way, and

26

Kirsten looked back at the house to see how far they'd come.

already her arms ached with fatigue. "Unless we work faster, we won't get to the barn before dark!" she said.

"If only we had another shovel instead of this pot," Lisbeth said. "If only Lars were—"

"Listen!" Kirsten said. "Did you hear a horse whinny?" She shaded her eyes against the glare off the snow. Blackie was struggling down the road through drifts up to his chest. Instead of the wagon, he was pulling a sleigh with Lars, Aunt Inger, and Mama in it!

Kirsten dropped the shovel. She and Lisbeth began to wave. They were crying and laughing at the same time. The others waved back. "They're safe!" Kirsten cried. "We're all safe! We stuck together and we made it through the blizzard!" Blackie whinnied again, as if he knew he was almost home.

JANET SHAW

At 8   Now

One spring when I was young, a snow-storm downed lots of power lines in my town. For several days we had no lights or heat in our house. It was exciting to read, eat, and sleep by the fireplace. It was like camping out! I was sorry when it was all over—but my mother was delighted!

Janet Shaw is the author of the Kirsten books in The American Girls Collection.

LOOKING
BACK
1854

A Peek Into
the Past

DEATH IN TH

MIDWEST BLASTED BY TERRIBLE BLIZZARD!

January 12, 1888, started out mild in the Midwest. I
seemed more like a spring day than a day in January
Children went to school without their coats. Me
worked in shirtsleeves.

But by midafternoon, howling winds and blindin
snow blasted huge areas of the region. Gusts rippe
roofs from houses, and small buildings were flattened.

The Schoolchildren's Storm

Some are calling the blizzard "The Schoolchildre
Storm." The violent storm trapped hundreds of child
and their teachers in schoolhouses across the Gr
Plains. Most teachers and their students escaped ha
Others weren't so lucky. There are reports that at l
200 men, women, and schoolchildren died during
Blizzard of 1888.

BIG STORM

NEBRASKA'S FEARLESS MAID

Nebraska teacher Miss Minnie May Freeman's calm and courage saved her students from the storm.

Miss Freeman knew the building would not last long, so she tied her students together with a ball of twine and led them to her home, nearly half a mile away.

"I thought of a ball of twine I had taken from a boy who was playing with it during class," said Miss Freeman. "I began tying the children together. Soon the roof blew off, and I said, 'Come on, children.'"

The teacher and the children trudged through the snow until they reached shelter. Some are calling Miss Freeman "Nebraska's Fearless Maid."

SOME LUCKY LAMBS

The day after the storm, one Nebraska farmer searched for his sheep. All he saw was a great cover of snow. He called and called to the sheep. At last he heard a muffled bleat and saw movement in the snow.

A tiny lamb popped its head out of the snowbank. As the farmer helped the lamb out, he discovered about a hundred more sheep under the snow. During the blizzard the sheep had put their heads under each other for warmth, and the snow had covered them and kept them snug and secure.

Digging Out

Some snowdrifts reached 20 feet.

CHILDREN'S CLOAKS-$6
Very pretty Child's Coat. Made of pla

Sisters Lost in the Storm

Two Nebraska sisters left school early to go home to their mother. They died in a snowdrift near their house. This poem was written in their memory:

"I can walk no further, sister, I am
Weary, cold, and worn. You go on, for
You are stronger; they will find me
In the morn." And she sank, benumbed
And weary, with a sobbing cry of woe,
Dying in the night and tempest;
Dying in the cruel snow.

"Try to walk a little further, soon
We'll see the gleaming light.
Let me fold my cloak around you."
But her sister, cold and white,
With a snowdrift for a pillow
Fell in dying sleep's repose,
While the snow came whirling, sifting,
Till above her form it rose.

Search in western song and story, and
Discover if you can, braver
Grander nobler action in the
History of man; than the silent

ALWAYS FAITHFUL

A Dakota man and his dog were lost in last week's storm. Rescuers found them close to home. The man was dead. His badly frozen dog was cuddled beside him. People say that the dog could have easily run to shelter—but it wouldn't leave its master behind in the bitter cold.

ACCIDENTS IN EVERY
SECTION OF CITY

COW SAVES GIRL!

On the morning of the blizzard, a Nebraska girl named Mary, age 11, set out to take her family's cows into a nearby field. The same old cow led the herd every day. When it was time to go back in, Mary would grab that cow's tail and it would start walking home. The other cows always followed.

When the blizzard struck, Mary was blinded by the snow. Thinking quickly, she grabbed the cow's tail. Even though it couldn't see, the cow knew its way home. Steady and sure, it led the girl and the herd to safety.

Cow is a hero!

Some people say the cow saved two lives—Mary's father was just about to go looking for her.

ALL THE STREETS
IMPASSABLE

The Cruel Work of Last Week's Blizzard

Blizzards rarely give any notice, and last week's was no exception. Travelers driving along under a clear sky one minute were caught the next in a swirl of snow that stung their faces like thousands of tiny needles.

Horses, unable to face the storm, turned from it, plunged into the snow, and never got up. Travelers didn't know what to do. Their bodies were numb with cold. They could see nothing and hear nothing. Soon they became exhausted trying to reach shelter. Many of these poor souls dropped down into the snow for a little rest, and the spark of life soon went out.

Nowhere to Hide

Many people were at risk during the storm—sometimes inside their own homes. When children and adults went to the woodshed for fuel, they tied ropes to the house and to themselves to make sure they could find their way back.

One can hardly imagine what it was like for those brave Dakota settlers who ran out of fuel for their fires. As the storm raged outside, temperatures in some areas of Dakota fell to 60 degrees below zero.

AN
AMERICAN
GIRLS
PASTIME

HAVE A SNOW DAY!

*Get ready for some
old-fashioned winter fun!*

When Kirsten and her family were
stuck inside during the blizzard, they
might have read a story to remind them
of their homeland or had fun making
shadow figures on the wall. After the
snow settled, they might have played
games on the snow-covered prairie.
Invite your friends over for some fun
in a winter wonderland.

Curl Up with a Snowy Story

Scandinavia is the part of Europe that includes Sweden, Denmark, and Norway. Kirsten and her cousins might have bundled up inside and read stories that reminded them of winters in Sweden. Hans Christian Andersen's tales are set in the landscape of Scandinavia. Stories like *The Snow Queen* are classics today, but they were brand-new in Kirsten's time. Look for a collection of other Hans Christian Andersen stories in your library.

Illustration from *The Snow Queen*

Warm Up with Spiced Chocolate

Spiced chocolate is a toasty drink for a cold day. Have an adult help you slowly heat 1 quart of milk in a saucepan. Stir it constantly until it boils. Put in 1 cinnamon stick and $1/3$ cup chocolate chips. Keep stirring. Let the mixture boil quickly, then turn off the heat. When the chocolate cools a bit, ask an adult to pour it into party mugs. Add cinnamon stick stirrers, if you wish.

Make Shadow Figures

Kirsten and her cousins may have been stuck inside, but they still had candlelight to make shadow figures on the wall. You can do the same with a flashlight. Shine a flashlight or an electric lamp directly toward a blank wall.

Make figures using the poses shown here. Then make up some figures of your own!

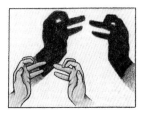

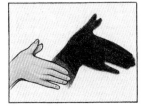

Play Fox and Geese

Fox and Geese was a wintertime favorite. It was Kirsten's version of tag.

Make a big circle in the snow with eight spokes across so that it looks like a huge wagon wheel. Choose one player to be the Fox. The other players are the Geese. The Fox chases the Geese up and down the spokes and around the outside rim of the circle. If a Goose reaches the middle of the circle, she is home free. When a Goose is tagged, she becomes the Fox.

No snow? Trace the wagon wheel in dirt or sand, or draw it with chalk.

Hop, Step, and Jump!

There was plenty of room for this game on the snow-covered prairie around Kirsten's cabin. Mark a line for a starting point. About ten feet away, mark another line. This is the "spring" line. The first player runs from the start line to the spring line. Then she hops three times on one leg, takes one long step, and finally makes the longest jump she can. The player to hop, step, and jump the farthest away from the spring line wins!